MR. HAPPY
finds a hobby

Original concept by Roger Hargreaves
Illustrated and written by Adam Hargreaves

World International

Mr Happy is a happy sort of fellow. He lives in Happyland which is a happy sort of place.

Behind his house there is a wood full of happy birds and on the other side of the wood there is a lake full of happy fish.

Now, one day, not that long ago, Mr Happy went for a walk through the wood.

As he came to the shore of the lake he heard an unusual sound.

A sound that is seldom heard in Happyland.

It was the sound of somebody moaning and grumbling.

Mr Happy peered round the trunk of a tree.

At the edge of the lake there was somebody fishing.

Fishing and grumbling.

And grumbling and fishing.

It was Mr Grumble.

"Good morning, Mr Grumble," said Mr Happy.

"Ssssh!" ssshed Mr Grumble.

"Sorry," whispered Mr Happy. "Have you caught anything?"

"Yes! I've caught a cold!" grumbled Mr Grumble.

"I've been sitting here all night. I hate fishing!"

"Then, why *are* you fishing?" asked Mr Happy.

"Because Mr Quiet said it was fun! And, you see, I'm trying to find something I enjoy doing. Something I can do as a hobby."

"Hmmm," pondered Mr Happy. "I might be able to help. Come on, let's see if we can find you a hobby."

As they walked along, Mr Happy thought long and hard and as he thought, Mr Grumble grumbled.

He grumbled about the noise the birds were making.

He grumbled about having to walk.

But most of all he grumbled about not having a hobby.

Grumble, grumble, grumble.

First of all they met Mr Rush in his car.
Mr Happy explained what they were doing.

"What's your hobby?" asked Mr Grumble.

"Speed!" said Mr Rush. "Hop in!"

And they did. Mr Grumble very quickly
decided that he did not like going fast.

Next they met Little Miss Giggles.

"What's your hobby?" asked Mr Grumble.

"I ... tee hee ... like ... tee hee ... giggling," giggled Miss Giggles.

So they went to the circus to see the clowns.

Little Miss Giggles giggled, Mr Happy laughed and Mr Grumble ... frowned!

"I hate custard pies," grumbled Mr Grumble.

It proved to be a very long day for Mr Happy.

They went everywhere.

They went to Little Miss Splendid's house.

But Mr Grumble did not like hats.

They went to Mr Mischief's house.
But Mr Grumble did not like practical jokes.

They bounced with Mr Bounce.

And they looked through keyholes with Mr Nosey.

But nothing was right. In fact, nothing was left.

Mr Happy had run out of ideas.

As the sun was setting they saw Mr Impossible coming towards them down the lane.

"Now, if anybody can help us that somebody ought to be Mr Impossible," said Mr Happy.

"Hello," Mr Happy said. "You're good at the impossible. Can you think of a hobby that Mr Grumble would enjoy?"

"That ... " said Mr Impossible.

"Yes ... " said Mr Happy and Mr Grumble together.

" ... would be impossible," said Mr Impossible.

"Grrr!" growled Mr Grumble, and stomped off home.

It was whilst drinking a cup of tea the next morning that Mr Happy had an idea.
A perfectly obvious idea.

He rushed round to Mr Grumble's house.

"I've got it!" cried Mr Happy. "You can take up fishing."

"Fishing?! But I hate fishing."

"I know, but what do you do while you are fishing?" asked Mr Happy.

"I don't know."

"You grumble," said Mr Happy. "And what do you like doing most of all?"

"I like ... " and then it dawned on Mr Grumble. "I like grumbling!"

Mr Grumble looked at Mr Happy and then, for the first time in a very long time, he smiled.

A very small smile, but a smile all the same.

Join Our Club!

MR. MEN
&
Little Miss
CLUB

When you become a member of the fantastic Mr Men and Little Miss Club you'll receive a personal letter from Mr Happy and Little Miss Giggles, a club badge with your name, and a superb Welcome Pack (pictured below right).

You'll also get birthday and Christmas cards from the Mr Men and Little Misses, 2 newsletters crammed with special offers, privileges and news, and a copy of the 12 page Mr Men catalogue which includes great party ideas.

If it were on sale in the shops, the Welcome Pack alone might cost around £13. But a year's membership is just £9.99 (plus 73p postage) with a 14 day money-back guarantee if you are not delighted!

HOW TO APPLY To apply for any of these three great offers, ask an adult to complete the coupon below and send it with appropriate payment and tokens (where required) to: Mr Men Offers, PO Box 7, Manchester M19 2HD. Credit card orders for Club membership ONLY by telephone, please call: 01403 242727.

To be completed by an adult

❏ **1.** Please send a poster and door hanger as selected overleaf. I enclose six tokens and a 50p coin for post (coin not required if you are also taking up 2. or 3. below).

❏ **2.** Please send ___ Mr Men Library case(s) and ___ Little Miss Library case(s) at £5.49 each.

❏ **3.** Please enrol the following in the Mr Men & Little Miss Club at £10.72 (inc postage)

Fan's Name._____Fan's Address:_____

_____Post Code:_____Date of birth: ___/___/___

Your Name:_____Your Address:_____

Post Code:_____Name of parent or guardian (if not you):_____

Total amount due: £_____ (£5.49 per Library Case, £10.72 per Club membership)

❏ I enclose a cheque or postal order payable to Egmont World Limited.

❏ Please charge my MasterCard / Visa account.

Card number: | | | | | | | | | | | | | | | | | |

Expiry Date: _____/_____   Signature: _____

Data Protection Act: If you do **not** wish to receive other family offers from us or companies we recommend, please tick this box ❏. Offer applies to UK only

3 Great Offers For Mr Men Fans

1 token EGMONT WORLD

1 FREE Door Hangers and Posters

In every Mr Men and Little Miss Book like this one you will find a special token. Collect 6 and we will send you either a brilliant Mr Men or Little Miss poster and a Mr Men or Little Miss double sided, full colour, bedroom door hanger. Apply using the coupon overleaf, enclosing six tokens and a 50p coin for your choice of two items.

Egmont World tokens can be used towards any other Egmont World / World International token scheme promotions, in early learning and story / activity books.

Posters: Tick your preferred choice of either Mr Men ☐ or Little Miss ☐

Door Hangers: Choose from: Mr. Nosey & Mr Muddle ☐, Mr Greedy & Mr Lazy ☐, Mr Tickle & Mr Grumpy ☐, Mr Slow & Mr Busy ☐, Mr Messy & Mr Quiet ☐, Mr Perfect & Mr Forgetful ☐, Little Miss Fun & Little Miss Late ☐, Little Miss Helpful & Little Miss Tidy ☐, Little Miss Busy & Little Miss Brainy ☐, Little Miss Star & Little Miss Fun ☐.
(Please tick)

2 Mr Men Library Boxes

Keep your growing collection of Mr Men and Little Miss books in these superb library boxes. With an integral carrying handle and stay-closed fastener, these full colour, plastic boxes are fantastic. They are just £5.49 each including postage. Order overleaf.

3 Join The Club

To join the fantastic Mr Men & Little Miss Club, check out the page overleaf NOW!

MR MEN and LITTLE MISS™ & © 1998 Mrs. Roger Hargreaves